The Seven Seas

Written by Ellen Jackson

Illustrated by Bill Slavin and Esperança Melo

Eerdmans Books for Young Readers

Grand Rapids, Michigan   •   Cambridge, U.K.

Text © 2011 Ellen Jackson
Illustrations © 2011 Bill Slavin and Esperança Melo

Published 2011 by Eerdmans Books for Young Readers
an imprint of Wm. B. Eerdmans Publishing Company
2140 Oak Industrial Dr. NE, Grand Rapids, Michigan 49505
P.O. Box 163, Cambridge CB3 9PU U.K.

Manufactured at Tien Wah Press in Singapore
August 2010, first printing

11 12 13 14 15 16 17   7 6 5 4 3 2 1

Library of Congress Cataloging-in-Publication Data

Jackson, Ellen B., 1943-
The seven seas / by Ellen Jackson; illustrated by Bill Slavin and Esperança Melo.
p. cm.
Summary: During a geography lesson, a child takes an imaginary journey to each of the seven seas,
including the Brown Sea which is made of chocolate, and the Pink Sea which has flamingos.
ISBN 978-0-8028-5341-7 (alk. paper)
[1. Stories in rhyme. 2. Seas — Fiction. 3. Geography — Fiction. 4. Imagination — Fiction. 5. Color — Fiction.]
I. Slavin, Bill, ill. II. Title.
PZ8.3.J1346Sev 2011
[E] — dc22
2010017730

The type is set in Gil Sans.
The illustrations were created with acrylics on gessoed paper.

To Sophia, Kiersten, and Bethany.
— *E.J.*

For Robin and James. May your lives be a voyage of discovery.
— *B.S. and E.M.*

My eyes were gazing at the map
when Mrs. Martin said,
"Now class, it's time to try to find
the Black Sea and the Red."

My mind began to wander
and everything was blurred.
The teacher kept on talking,
but I didn't hear a word.

I thought I saw the seven seas;
I wanted to explore.
I went by train, by boat, by plane,
and gazed on every shore.

I took a bus to Marrakesh,

a taxi to Peru.

I rode a mule to Istanbul,

a yak to Timbuktu.

The Yellow Sea's a mystery,
a sight that's worth the trip.
They say it's made of lemonade
and quite all right to sip.

The Green Sea has a rocky reef,
where caterpillars crawl,
and near your toes the broccoli grows
until it's twelve feet tall.

The Red Sea looks like pizza sauce —
a little or a lottle.
The roosters dine on ladybugs
with ketchup from a bottle.

The Brown Sea's made of chocolate,
a place to drown your cares.
Its whipped cream foam is home sweet home
to brownish, clownish bears.

The Black Sea's made of licorice,
and daylight's never seen.
With bats and cats and skeletons,
it's always Halloween!

The Purple Sea serves royalty,
where queens and kings can wade.
And angry princes hold their breath
to turn a purplish shade.

The Pink Sea has flamingos
and cotton candy clouds,
and rows and rows of sunburned toes
on sandal-wearing crowds.

"Class, you're dismissed," the teacher said,
while rolling up the chart.

SNAP!!!

Then from my head the daydreams fled,
and gave me quite a start.

Oh, I have seen the seven seas,
in every shade and hue.
But when I finally looked at them,
they all were colored . . .

Yes, I have seen the seven seas,
I've checked them off my list.
Can you surmise which ones are lies,
and which of them exist?

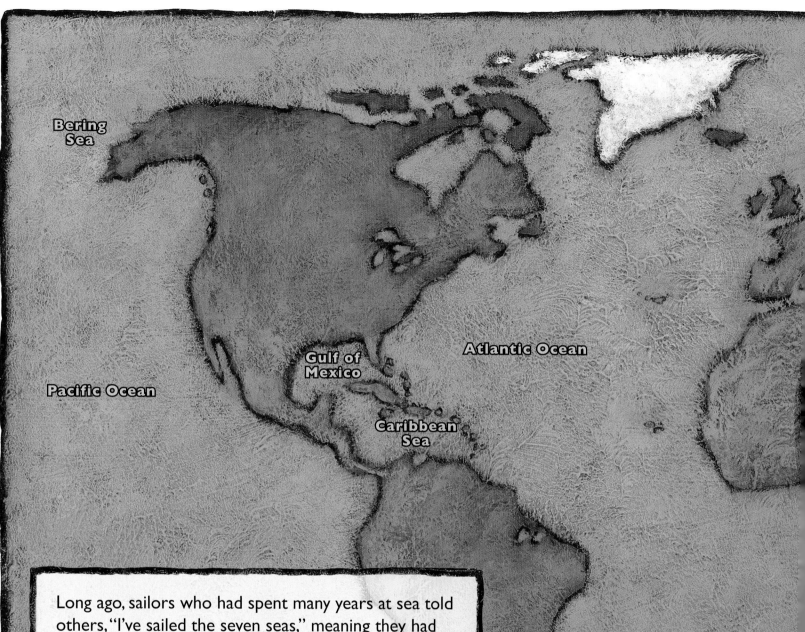

Bering
Sea

Atlantic Ocean

Pacific Ocean

Gulf of
Mexico

Caribbean
Sea

Southern Ocean

Long ago, sailors who had spent many years at sea told others, "I've sailed the seven seas," meaning they had been all over the world. By the Middle Ages, the "seven seas" most often referred to the Red Sea, the Mediterranean Sea, the Persian Gulf, the Black Sea, the Adriatic Sea, the Caspian Sea, and the Indian Ocean.

The seven seas described in this book are imaginary, but three of them have the same name as real places. Can you identify which of these seas are real?

What is a sea?

A sea is a body of salt water that is at least partly surrounded by land. Today, over fifty bodies of water are called seas, though often the words *sea* and *ocean* are used interchangeably.

All oceans and seas in the world are part of one huge body of water that covers more than 70% of the earth's surface. Because this mass of water is so big, people have named different parts of it. For example, you may have heard of the Pacific Ocean or the Atlantic Ocean. There are no clear boundaries between these oceans: they flow into one another. You will not see a sign when you cross from one ocean to another.

Use the map to find the world's largest oceans and seas:

Pacific Ocean
Atlantic Ocean
Indian Ocean
Southern Ocean
Arctic Ocean
South China Sea
Caribbean Sea
Mediterranean Sea
Bering Sea
Gulf of Mexico

Additional Resources

Berkes, Marianne. *Over in the Ocean: In a Coral Reef.* CA: Dawn Publications, 2004.
Burns, Loree Griffin. *Tracking Trash: Flotsam, Jetsam, and the Science of Ocean Motion.* MA: Houghton Mifflin, 2007.
Daynes, Katie. *1001 Things to Spot in the Sea.* MN: Usborne Books, 2003.
Dinwiddie, Robert, et al. *Ocean: The World's Last Wilderness Revealed.* NY: DK Publishing, 2006.
Priddy, Roger. *Big and Busy Ocean.* NY: St. Martin's Press, 2009.

Fun Facts about Seas and Oceans

Why do seas and oceans look blue?

The ocean usually appears blue because that is the color that reaches our eyes. Sunlight is made up of all the colors in the rainbow, but water reflects more blue rays and absorbs the other colors, so our eyes see the blue.

If seas and oceans look blue, why are they given names of different colors?

The names for seas and oceans come from many different places. For instance, the Red Sea contains a red-colored algae that blooms near its surface. But no one is exactly sure where this sea got its name; it may also have come from reddish mountains nearby or the name of a group of people who lived near the sea long ago.

The Yellow Sea is a fitting name because this sea does look yellow — at least at sunset, when the sea turns a golden color from the sand blown into it from the Gobi Desert.

The Black Sea doesn't actually look black, and it's not really made of licorice! It may have gotten its name because it contains a naturally occurring chemical that produces black sediment. The name may also be from an old Turkish word for north.

Why is seawater salty?

The salt in seawater comes from rocks on land. Water and acids dissolve this material in the rocks, and rivers carry it to the sea. Some seas are saltier than others. When a sea is warm, more water evaporates from the surface, leaving the salt behind.

What is the warmest sea to swim in?

The warmest sea is the Red Sea. Its temperatures reach 88°F (31°C). But the water in the Persian Gulf has gotten even warmer than that. It sometimes reaches 95°F (35°C) on the surface — that would feel like your bathwater!

What's the biggest ocean in the world?

The Pacific Ocean is the largest and deepest ocean in the world. It holds about half of all the water on Earth. When the explorer Ferdinand Magellan sailed around the world in 1519, he named this ocean "Pacific," which means calm or peaceful. But the Pacific Ocean is not always a peaceful place. Thousands of volcanoes rise out of its waters, and typhoons and hurricanes rage across its surface.

Is the Dead Sea really dead?

The Dead Sea gets its name because it is so salty that most living creatures and plants cannot live in its water. If you go swimming in the Dead Sea, you can float on the surface with no effort at all because all the salt and minerals in it make you more buoyant.

How deep is the ocean?

The lowest point on earth is over 35,000 feet (almost 11,000 meters) deep in the western Pacific Ocean, in a place called the Mariana Trench. This trench is so deep that the highest mountain in the world would fit into it!

What's the biggest wave ever?

The tallest wave ever to reach shore was off the coast of Alaska. It was 1720 feet (524 meters) high, taller than any building in the United States!

Some people say the ocean glows at night. Does it really?

If you spend time on the ocean at night, you may see a glow or sparkling light in the waves. This light is caused by tiny creatures whose bodies contain a substance that glows in the dark. This is similar to the way that fireflies light up on a summer night. Deep down in the ocean where it's very dark, many creatures glow with this same blue-green light, and some produce a red light.